Story and Pictures by

Judith Vigna

Albert Whitman & Company, Chicago

SECOND PRINTING 1975

Library of Congress Cataloging in Publication Data

Vigna, Judith.
Gregory's stitches.

SUMMARY: The story of how Gregory got the six stitches in his forehead changes with each friend that passes on the news.

I. Title.
PZ7.V67Gr [E] 73-22400
ISBN 0-8075-3046-8

Published simultaneously in Canada by
George J. McLeod, Limited, Toronto

One day
a *terrible* thing
happened to Gregory.

He had to go to the doctor
and have six stitches put
in his forehead.

Not three.
Not four.
But *six!*

Coming out of the doctor's office,
Gregory saw his friend John.

4652

“What happened?” asked John.

“I fell off my bike,” said Gregory.

John met David.
"Guess what?" he said.
"Gregory was chased by a dog
and fell off his bike
and got *six* stitches
in his forehead."

David sped away to tell Michael.

"Did you hear about Gregory?"
he asked.
"He was climbing a tree
to rescue a kitten
that was chased by a dog
and got six stitches
in his *forehead!*"

Michael ran over to Freddie's.
"Know what?" Michael asked.

"Gregory got attacked
by a big dog
that was chasing his cat
and got six *stitches*
in his forehead!"

Freddie passed the word to Albert.
"Gregory got *six* stitches
in his forehead!
He was rescuing a kitten
that fell into the wild dog's cage
at the zoo."

Albert told Jimmy.
"Did you hear what happened to Gregory?
He went to the zoo with his parents
and got mauled by a *lion*
and got six stitches in his forehead!"

Jimmy couldn't wait
to tell his friend Jenny.
"Guess what Gregory did!
He saved his parents
from being killed
by some man-eating lions
at the zoo
and got *six stitches* in his forehead!"

So everyone who knew about Gregory
hurried off to Gregory's house.

Gregory was at home,
with a big Band-Aid on his forehead.

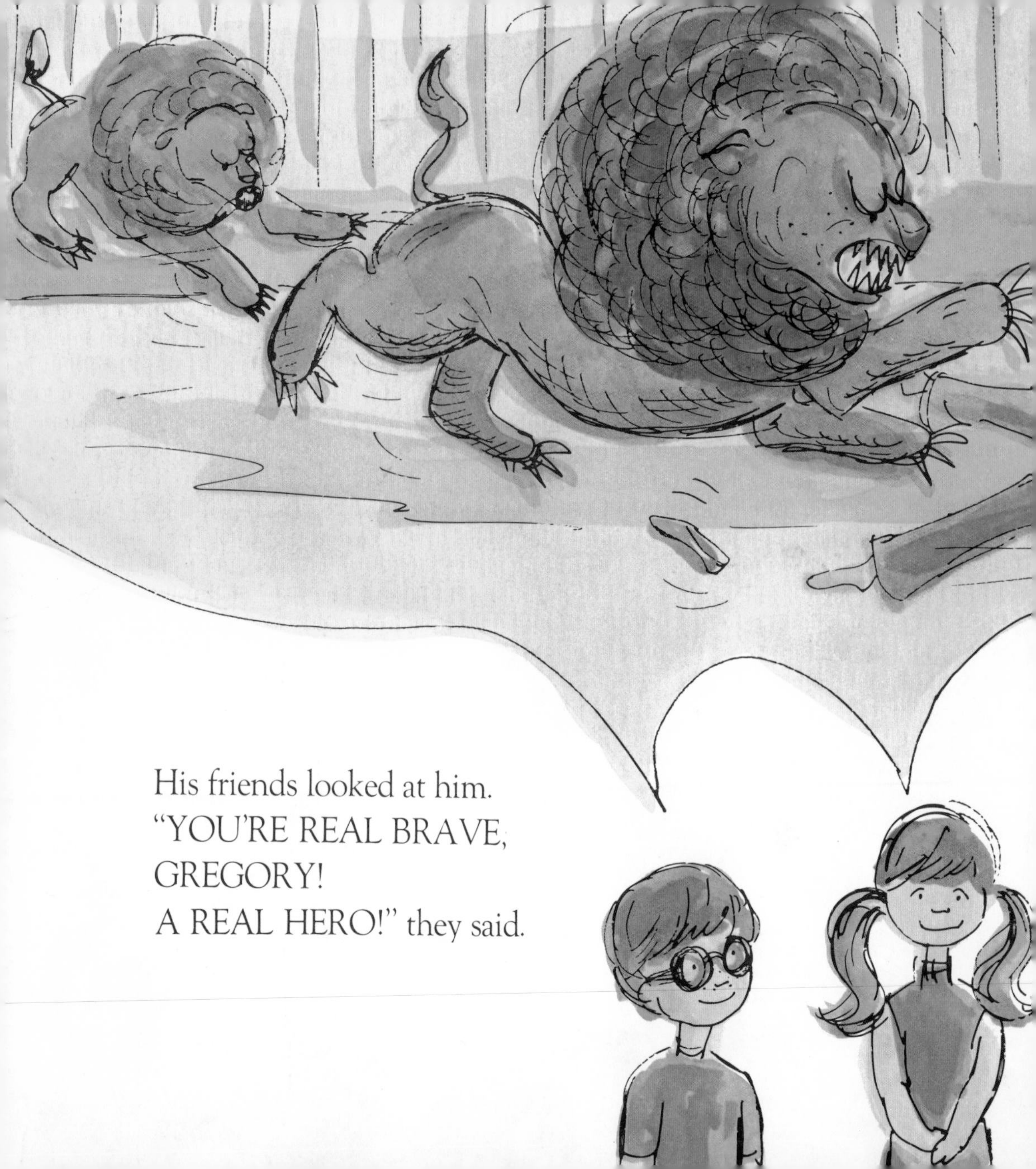

His friends looked at him.
"YOU'RE REAL BRAVE,
GREGORY!
A REAL HERO!" they said.

And getting stitches didn't seem so terrible after all.

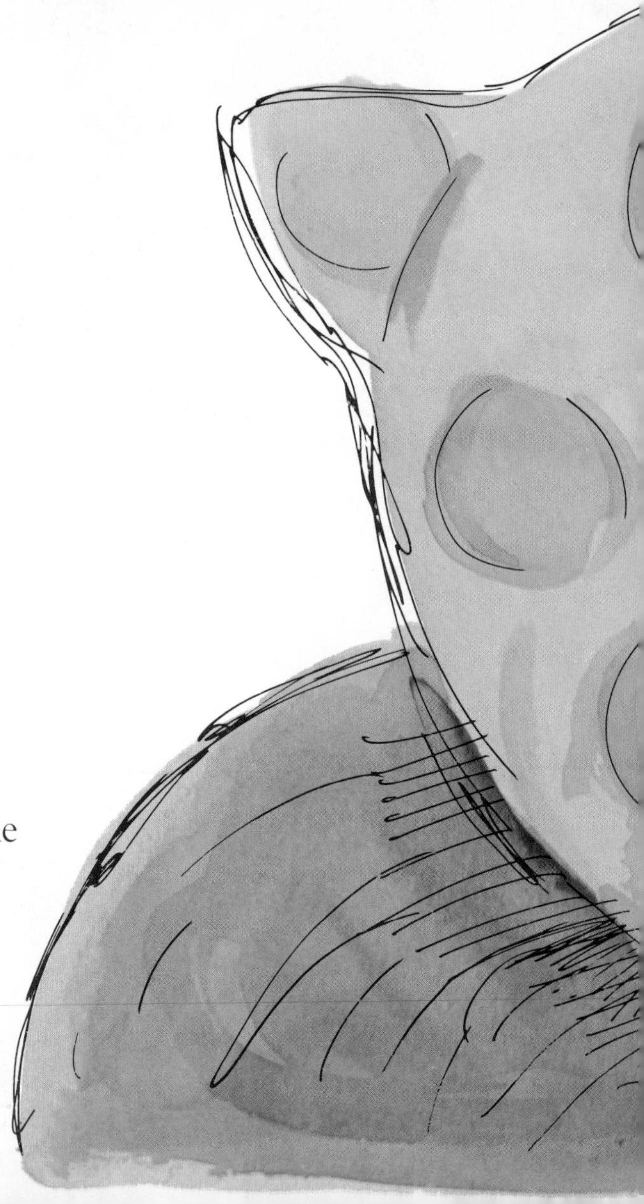

Judith Vigna spent her childhood years in England, where she was born. Even as a child, she enjoyed drawing and writing poetry and stories, and she remembers early ambitions to be an artist-writer. Art training in London and in New York led to newspaper and public relations work, then to advertising writing.

Now living in New York, Judith Vigna is completing a degree in art therapy, hoping to apply her skills to work with emotionally disturbed children. Professional portrait painting is another interest, and her oils and watercolors have been exhibited in local art shows.

Gregory's Stitches is the author's first book for children. Anyone who's ever had stitches can empathize with Gregory, and his story lends itself to elaboration and acting out.